Fancy NANCY Puppy Party

Based on *Fancy Nancy* written by Jane O'Connor

Cover illustration by Robin Preiss Glasser

Interior illustrations by Carolyn Bracken

HARPER FESTIVAL
An Imprint of HarperCollinsPublishers

HarperFestival is an imprint of HarperCollins Publishers.

Fancy Nancy: Puppy Party
Text copyright © 2013 by Jane O'Connor
Illustrations copyright © 2013 by Robin Preiss Glasser
Manufactured in China. All rights reserved.
No part of this book may be used or reproduced in any manner whatsoever without written permission except in the case of brief quotations embodied in critical articles and reviews.
For information address HarperCollins Children's books, a division of HarperCollins Publishers, 195 Broadway, New York, NY 10007.
www.harpercollinschildrens.com
Library of Congress catalog card number: 2012944108
ISBN 978-0-06-208627-3
Book design by Sean Boggs
16 17   SCP   10 9 8 7
❖
First Edition

Tomorrow is Frenchy's birthday.
We are having a huge celebration.
(That's a fancy word for party.)

All Frenchy's canine—that means dog—friends are coming.
Their owners get to come too.

Of course, the birthday girl must look *extra exquisite* for the party, so Frenchy gets a bubble bath.

Then my dad tries to clip Frenchy's nails.

She is not very fond of getting her nails clipped.

Later I brush her fur until it's gleaming—that's fancy for shiny.

I spray her with special doggy perfume called Eau de Woof Woof.

Mmmm. Frenchy smells so fragrant now!

The next morning, we all help bake a bacon-chicken-carrot layer cake. That's Frenchy's favorite.

My favorite is chocolate, but dogs can't digest chocolate. That means if they eat it, they get sick and throw up.

The frosting on Frenchy's cake is yogurt, and for candles we use rawhide strings.

Voilà! All done.

Soon the guests begin to arrive. Frenchy greets each one of them. I am almost positive she's barking in French.

Mrs. DeVine's dog, Jewel, looks nearly as fancy as Mrs. DeVine. Mrs. DeVine and Jewel even wear matching hair clips!

Bree and Freddy bring their dog, Rusty.

Sam and Scamp come too.

So does my babysitter, Alex, and his beagle, Buddy.

We give all the guests party hats. Scamp tries to eat hers!

The party is a *sensational* success!
Frenchy is a wonderful hostess.

She lets the other dogs share her balls and tug toys.

Soon it's cake time. We all sing "Happy Birthday" to Frenchy as Mom brings in the cake.

Uh-oh! Frenchy can't resist lunging at the cake.
Mom drops it, and Frenchy lands on top of it!

The other dogs jump on the cake too. It's total pandemonium!
(That means all the dogs go wild!)

The birthday girl does NOT look fancy anymore!
She is covered in yogurt and cake. So are all the other dogs.
I start to reprimand Frenchy. (That's fancy for scold.)

But then I see that everyone is laughing.
I start giggling too.

After we wash off all the dogs, Frenchy comes over and licks my face. She barks and wags her tail.

She is telling me this was the greatest birthday celebration ever!